WILLIE
Comes Home

Willie Rejoins the Fairmont Bears

AuthorHouse™
1663 Liberty Drive
Bloomington, IN 47403
www.authorhouse.com
Phone: 833-262-8899

This book is printed on acid-free paper.

ISBN: 978-1-6655-7467-9 (sc)
ISBN: 978-1-6655-7466-2 (e)

Library of Congress Control Number: 2022920084

Print information available on the last page.

Published by AuthorHouse   11/14/2022

authorHOUSE

WILLIE
COMES HOME

"I am so dizzy!" Willy exclaimed with a slur. Willie found himself laying beside the train tracks, but was so very confused.

As he slowly got up on all fours and headed into the woods, he remembered what Mama always said: "Shake it off Willie; Shake it off!" So that's just what he did - Shake Shake Shake

He looked around for his brother Miles and his mom Millie, but could not see either of them. "They must have wandered off deeper into the mountains. I will just have to catch up to them" he said confidently.

Things went pretty good for a while, as there were still some dandelions

and tender green grasses
to munch on.

But then, as spring turned to summer, and the dandelions went to seed, there was not as much easy food to eat. Willie got skinnier and skinnier and sadder and sadder. He missed his mom and brother soooo... much. Willie spent his days walking along-side the highway and sometimes he wandered deeper into the forest where he felt safer, but Willie felt so alone.

Willie bumped into many different animals along the way as he searched for his family; some were scary, some stinky, some majestic, but nobody looked quite like him.

Willie just about bumped into a monster-sized moose. The moose seemed to like the swampy part of the forest.

Then a very gangly goat wandered down from a very steep part of the mountain. Willie admired his sure-footedness on the slippery slope.

As he carried on, a strong odor filled the fresh mountain air. It happened to be a stinky skunk with its family living in the culvert. Willie sojourned on even with his eyes stinging from putting his snout too deep into the culvert. "I won't do that again!", he said to himself. It just goes to show you shouldn't stick your nose into someone else's business.

19

Then Willie looked up, and a lone wandering wolf stood proud on the mountain. Even with his sore weak eyes, Willie could see the beautiful colors of the wolf against the bright blue sky.

Willie just about bumped into a Radium ram; "Oops" he mumbled to himself.

Willie was careful to avoid the large grizzly. He crawled high into a tree until danger passed.

Willie did not give up all summer long. Soon, there were very delicious berries to eat – the last of the ripe red raspberries, orange buffalo berries, purple chokecherries. Yum!

Now there was enough food for everyone, including the birds flying tree to tree.

Finally, full to the brim and very, very sleepy, Willie yawned and yawned as he wandered higher and higher on the mountain slope. Something was drawing him back to the ski hill, he was not sure why, but he ventured on. It was already very chilly and snowy this high up.

Suddenly, Willie lifted his snout high, and smelled something very familiar. He knew that smell. Being curious he entered a den, and who do you think was there?

It was Mom Millie and his brother Miles. They were both fast asleep. Willie carefully snuggled up to them, and sighed – "Home". After all, even a small black bear knows home is where your family is. With one last yawn, Willie fell soundly asleep. He felt so safe.

After arising in the spring and in the months that followed, it was just like old times, the family of bears did what Fairmont bears do – lots of climbing, wandering through yards, eating whatever fancies them, and doing whatever they please. They were indeed one happy family.

We do love our bears!

Willie asks that you finish this picture of him in the forest.

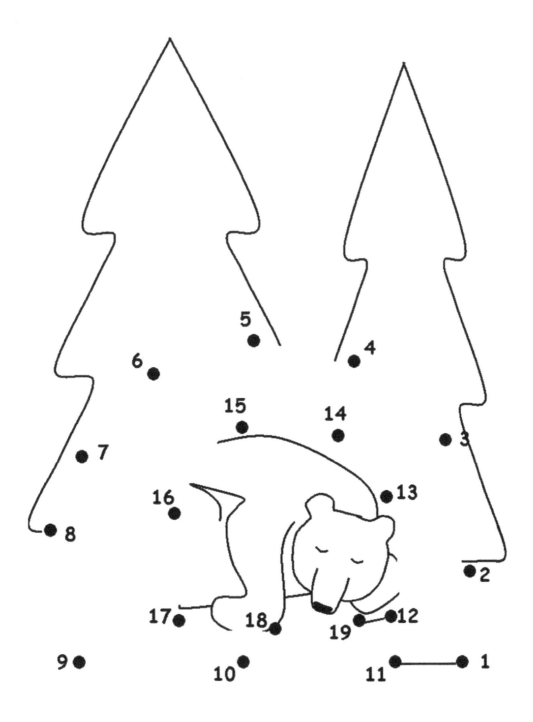

The End